The Animals' Football Cup

by Clare De Marco and Trevor Dunton

W
FRANKLIN WATTS
LONDON•SYDNEY

First published in 2011 by
Franklin Watts
338 Euston Road
London
NW1 3BH

Franklin Watts Australia
Level 17/207 Kent Street
Sydney
NSW 2000

Text © Clare De Marco 2011
Illustration © Trevor Dunton 2011

The rights of Clare De Marco to be identified as the
author and Trevor Dunton as the illustrator of this Work have been
asserted in accordance with the Copyright, Designs and
Patents Act, 1988.

A CIP catalogue record for this book is available
from the British Library.

ISBN 978 0 7496 9471 5 (hbk)
ISBN 978 0 7496 9477 7 (pbk)

Series Editor: Jackie Hamley
Series Advisor: Catherine Glavina
Series Designer: Peter Scoulding

Printed in China

Franklin Watts is a divison of
Hachette Children's Books,
an Hachette UK company.
www.hachette.co.uk

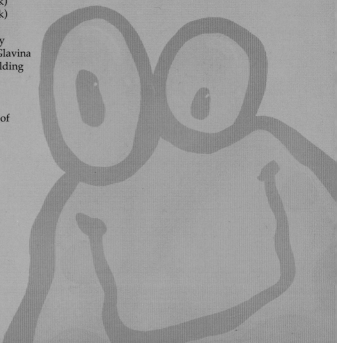

It was the day of the football cup final.

JUNGLE UNITED

RAINFOREST ROVERS

3

Jungle United were excited.

"I'm fierce," roared Lion.

"I'll stop the other team."

"I'm tall," said Giraffe. "I'll head the ball into the goal."

"I'm nimble," said Gazelle.
"I'll kick the ball to Giraffe."

Hippo said nothing.
"I'm not good at anything,"
he thought.

The Rainforest Rovers
team arrived. They were
fast and strong.

Monkey blew his whistle to start the game.

Hippo didn't play well.
First, he stood on Giraffe.

Then Hippo scored an own goal by mistake.

"I'm too big and clumsy,"
thought Hippo, sadly.
Gazelle had an idea.

"You're big," she said. "You can be the goalkeeper!" Hippo smiled.

Soon Lion roared past the other team and scored.

"1-1" shouted Monkey.

Then Gazelle kicked the ball high and Giraffe headed it in.

20

"2-1 to Jungle United!" shouted Monkey.

But in the last minute,
Lion tripped up a
Rainforest Rovers player.

"Penalty!" shouted Monkey.

Hippo shook in his goal as the player ran up to take the penalty …

… but the ball bounced straight off Hippo's bottom!

Monkey blew his whistle.
"Jungle United win!"

"Three cheers for Hippo!"

Puzzle 1

Put these pictures in the correct order.
Now tell the story in your own words.
How short can you make the story?

clumsy   large

tiny

shy   fierce

strong

Choose the words which best describe each character. Can you think of any more? Pretend to be one of the characters!

Answers

Puzzle 1

The correct order is:

1d, 2e, 3b, 4a, 5f, 6c

Puzzle 2

Hippo   The correct words are clumsy, large.
The incorrect word is tiny.

Lion   The correct words are fierce, strong.
The incorrect word is shy.

Look out for more Leapfrog stories:

The Little Star
ISBN 978 0 7496 3833 7

Mary and the Fairy
ISBN 978 0 7496 9142 4

Jack's Party
ISBN 978 0 7496 4389 8

Pippa and Poppa
ISBN 978 0 7496 9140 0

The Bossy Cockerel
ISBN 978 0 7496 9141 7

The Best Snowman
ISBN 978 0 7496 9143 1

Big Bad Blob
ISBN 978 0 7496 7092 4*
ISBN 978 0 7496 7796 1

Cara's Breakfast
ISBN 978 0 7496 7797 8

Croc's Tooth
ISBN 978 0 7496 7799 2

The Magic Word
ISBN 978 0 7496 7800 5

Tim's Tent
ISBN 978 0 7496 7801 2

Why Not?
ISBN 978 0 7496 7798 5

Sticky Vickie
ISBN 978 0 7496 7986 6

Handyman Doug
ISBN 978 0 7496 7987 3

Billy and the Wizard
ISBN 978 0 7496 7985 9

Sam's Spots
ISBN 978 0 7496 7984 2

Bill's Baggy Trousers
ISBN 978 0 7496 3829 0

Bill's Bouncy Shoes
ISBN 978 0 7496 7990 3

Bill's Scary Backpack
ISBN 978 0 7496 9458 6*
ISBN 978 0 7496 9468 5

Little Joe's Big Race
ISBN 978 0 7496 3832 0

Little Joe's Balloon Race
ISBN 978 0 7496 7989 7

Little Joe's Boat Race
ISBN 978 0 7496 9457 9*
ISBN 978 0 7496 9467 8

Felix on the Move
ISBN 978 0 7496 4387 4

Felix and the Kitten
ISBN 978 0 7496 7988 0

Felix Takes the Blame
ISBN 978 0 7496 9456 2*
ISBN 978 0 7496 9466 1

The Cheeky Monkey
ISBN 978 0 7496 3830 6

Cheeky Monkey on Holiday
ISBN 978 0 7496 7991 0

Cheeky Monkey's Treasure Hunt
ISBN 978 0 7496 9455 5*
ISBN 978 0 7496 9465 4

For details of all our titles go to: www.franklinwatts.co.uk

*hardback